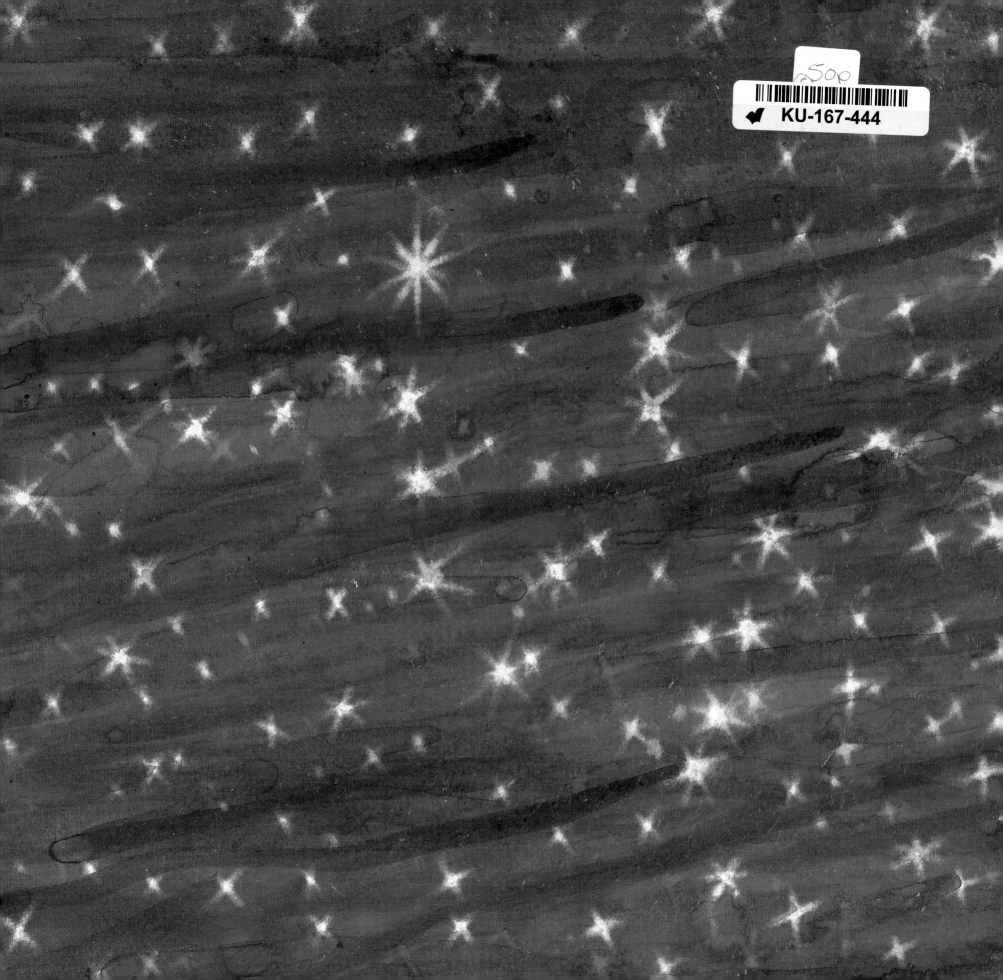

For Janet and Cedric, Peter and Ben, and most especially Marc.
And thank you Giulietta and Serena.

My story is inspired by the Arctic National Wildlife Refuge in Alaska. The Arctic Refuge protects twenty million acres of wilderness and is the wildest and most free of human influences and intrusion of all national wildlife refuges. I feel comforted by the knowledge that this is a safe place, a heaven on earth, for endangered animals. To quote Supreme Court Justice William O. Douglas, 'This last American living wilderness must remain sacrosanct'.

P H

First published in 2002 by
Orion Children's Books
a division of the Orion Publishing Group Ltd
Orion House
5 Upper St Martin's Lane
London WC2H 9EA

Printed and bound in Italy

Polly and the North Star

Polly Horner

Orion
Children's Books

Polly's father was going on an expedition. He was going far, far away to Alaska where wolves and polar bears live.

Polly was crying. She didn't want him to go. She was afraid he would never come back.

"I must go, Polly," her father said. "I have to help the animals. But I will always be with you. Before you go to sleep, look out of the window and follow the Great Bear in the sky. It will lead you to the North Star. Wherever I am, I will be doing the same, and when we both reach the star we will say goodnight to each other."

At bedtime Polly liked to read to Sirius, her wolfdog, about the animals and places her father was trying to protect, and together they imagined him leading the animals out of danger.

And every night before they went to sleep Polly and Sirius looked out of the window and followed the Great Bear till they came to the North Star. Then Polly closed her eyes and said, "Goodnight, Daddy, wherever you are."

Then Polly would dream that she and Sirius were in Alaska with her father.

Her father introduced them to his friends the animals.
Polly met polar bears, grey wolves, snowy owls and caribou.

She made special friends with a polar bear she called
Snowflake, and a snowy owl she called Mercury.

Polly's favourite dream was when she and her father and Sirius had a moonlight picnic with the animals.

Polly's dreams made her happy, but she still
counted the days until her father was coming home.
And when the day came, she was so busy and excited that
she didn't notice it was starting to snow.

At bedtime her father had still not arrived. Polly looked out of the window and saw that the snow had turned into a blizzard. She couldn't see the North Star. She knew her father was in trouble.

She closed her eyes and wished with all her heart that she could be with him and bring him home safely.

When she opened her eyes again, Polly was standing
in a raging blizzard, with Sirius beside her.

"Sirius," cried Polly,
"we have to find Daddy!"

They tried to walk but the snow was very deep
and the storm was very fierce.

Sirius raised his head
and howled.

Then out of the blizzard came Polly's friends the animals.
"Snowflake! Mercury!" cried Polly. She climbed on Snowflake's back.
Far away a bright light shone above the forest. The animals took Polly towards it.

It was the North Star shining down on a clearing in the forest

where Polly's father lay in the snow.

Polly ran and helped him up. "It's all right, Daddy!
We've come to take you home!" she cried.

Then Polly woke up. She was at home in bed, with her father's arms around her and Sirius at her side.

"I'm back, Polly," said her father.

"Welcome home, Daddy," said Polly, and gave him a great big hug.

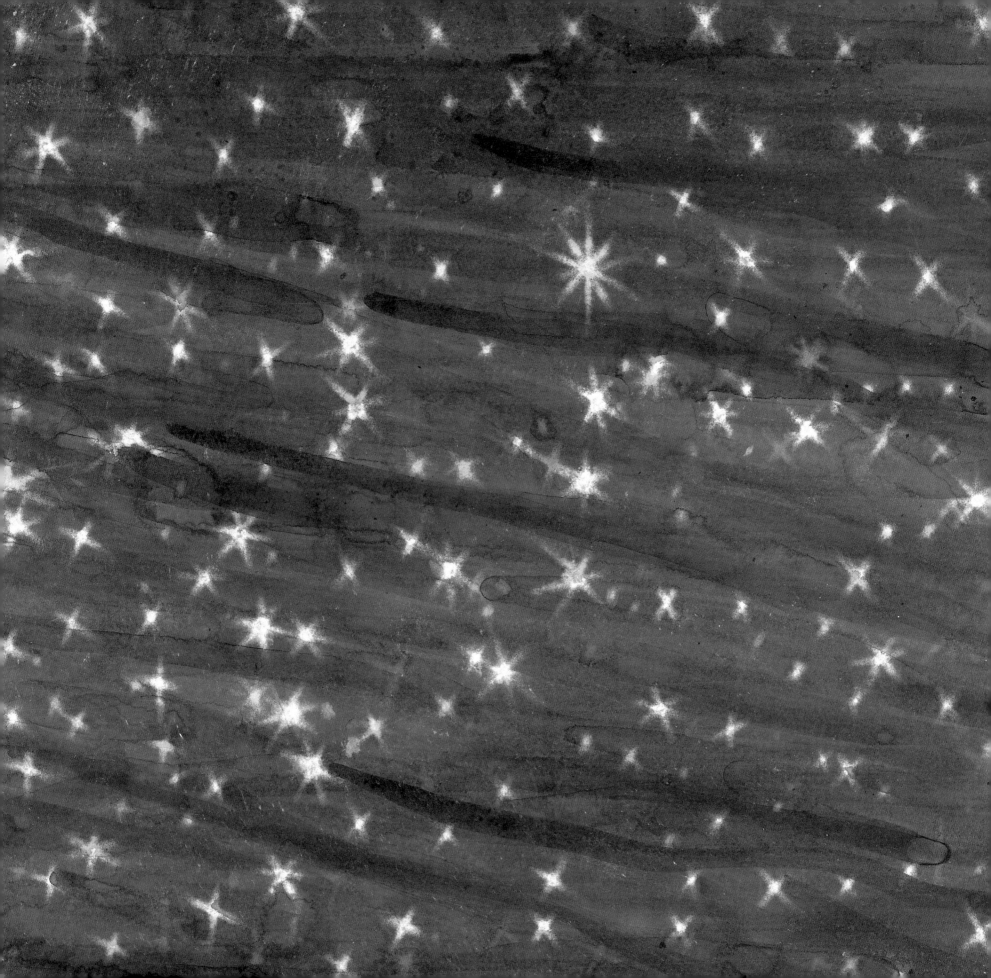